FOREST OF FAITH

A Christmas Tree for JESUS

Celebrating God's Gift to Us

by Susan Jones

Illustrated by Lee Holland

Good  Books

New York, New York

Whispers of excited voices float
into the Mouse family burrow.
Curious Little Mouse pops out of bed.

"What's going on?" asks Little Mouse.

"Some of our forest friends are choosing the tree we will decorate for our Christmas celebration," Mama Mouse explains.

The Mouse family isn't
the only one up and about.

"Now that everyone is ready to greet the day, who has ideas for how we will decorate our tree this year?" asks Grandma Turtle.

"Let's make it all purple,"
suggests Little Hedgehog.

"Oooh, I know, a cookie tree!"
shouts Little Bunny.

"What if we each add an ornament that celebrates something amazing about Jesus?" suggests Grandma Turtle.

Everyone thinks this is a great idea.

Chatting excitedly, the friends
scurry, hop, and *fly* home to
get started on their ornaments.

But Little Mouse walks slowly,
quietly at the back of the pack.

The next day the decorating team gathers at the Christmas tree.

"Who is ready to add an ornament?" asks Grandma Turtle.

Some friends jump up and run to the tree. But where is Little Mouse?

"I brought a *fish* because Jesus made two *fish* and *five* loaves of bread *feed* more than 5,000 people," says Little Skunk.

"This manger reminds us that Jesus came to earth as a tiny baby," shares Little Bunny.

"Here is a sheep, for Jesus our shepherd," says Little Chipmunk.

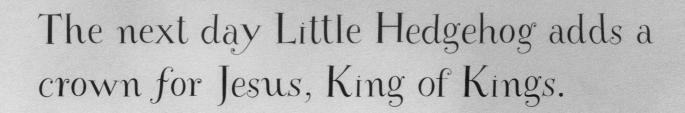

The next day Little Hedgehog adds a crown for Jesus, King of Kings.

Little Raccoon shares a butterfly for new life found through Jesus.

And Little Bird brings a small bouquet of herbs because Jesus heals.

Little Mouse feels worried. What can she offer?

"What's wrong?" asks Grandma Turtle.

"I have no ornament to share," Little Mouse says. "I don't know what to do."

Grandma Turtle puts her arm around Little Mouse. "Let me tell you a secret. One of the most amazing things about Jesus is that He is with us today and every day."

Just then, Little Mouse gets an idea.
As his friends call after him, he
runs home to get to work.

Little Mouse works the rest of the day on his ornament and a surprise *for his friends.*

The next day, Little Mouse can hardly wait to put his ornament on the tree.

"Show us," Grandma and the friends encourage him.

"I made a heart because it's so amazing that Jesus loves me, knows me, and came to earth *for me* on Christmas," says Little Mouse.

"And that's true for all of us,
so I made a heart for each of you!"

"The Christmas tree is ready just in time for our birthday celebration for Jesus!" says Little Mouse.

"And you've already discovered the best gift: how Jesus knows and loves each and every one of us!" says Grandma Turtle.

Good Books books may be purchased in bulk at special discounts for sales promotion, corporate gifts, fund-raising, or educational purposes. Special editions can also be created to specifications. For details, contact the Special Sales Department, Good Books, 307 West 36th Street, 11th Floor, New York, NY 10018 or info@skyhorsepublishing.com.

Good Books is an imprint of Skyhorse Publishing, Inc.®, a Delaware corporation.

Visit our website at www.goodbooks.com.

10 9 8 7 6 5 4 3 2 1

Library of Congress Cataloging-in-Publication Data

Names: Jones, Susan (Devotional writer), author. | Holland, Lee
   (Illustrator), illustrator.
Title: A Christmas tree for Jesus : celebrating God's gift to us / by Susan
   Jones ; illustrated by Lee Holland.
Description: New York : Good Books, 2021. | Series: Forest of faith |
   Audience: Ages 4-8 | Audience: Grades K-1 | Summary: Forest animals add
   handmade ornaments to their community's tree and Little Mouse looks
   inside herself to understand a deeper meaning of Christmas.
Identifiers: LCCN 2021018784 (print) | LCCN 2021018785 (ebook) | ISBN
   9781680997538 (hardcover) | ISBN 9781680997736 (epub)
Subjects: CYAC: Christian life--Fiction. | Christmas--Fiction. | Forest
   animals--Fiction. | Animals--Fiction.
Classification: LCC PZ7.1.J746 Ch 2021 (print) | LCC PZ7.1.J746 (ebook) |
   DDC [E]--dc23
LC record available at https://lccn.loc.gov/2021018784
LC ebook record available at https://lccn.loc.gov/2021018785

Cover design by Katie Jennings
Cover illustration by Lee Holland

Print ISBN: 978-1-68099-753-8
Ebook ISBN: 978-1-68099-773-6

Printed in China